THIS WALKER BOOK BELONGS TO:

For Peter

L.V.

First published 1988 by Walker Books Ltd
87 Vauxhall Walk, London SE11 5HJ

This edition published 2003

2 4 6 8 10 9 7 5 3

This book has been typeset in Garamond

Printed in China

British Library Cataloguing in Publication Data:
a catalogue record for this book is available from the British Library

ISBN 0-7445-9801-X

Hello, Goodbye

David Lloyd

illustrated by

Louise Voce

WALKER BOOKS
AND SUBSIDIARIES
LONDON • BOSTON • SYDNEY

A tree stood quietly
in the sunshine.

Hello!

A big brown bear stepped up.
"Hello!" he said, very loudly.

hello!
hello!

Two bees flew over.
"Hello! Hello!" they said, very busily.

Along came a big red bird.
What did the bird say?
"Hello!" – very quickly.

Soon voices all over the tree were saying, "Hello!"

hello

Deep-down voices among the roots said, "Hello!"

hello
hello.
hello
hello
hello!
hello
hello.

Suddenly
a drop of rain fell
on the bear's nose.
Splash!

Raindrops fell all over the bear.
Splash! Splash! Splash!

Goodbye!
goodbye
goodbye...
goodbye
goodbye!

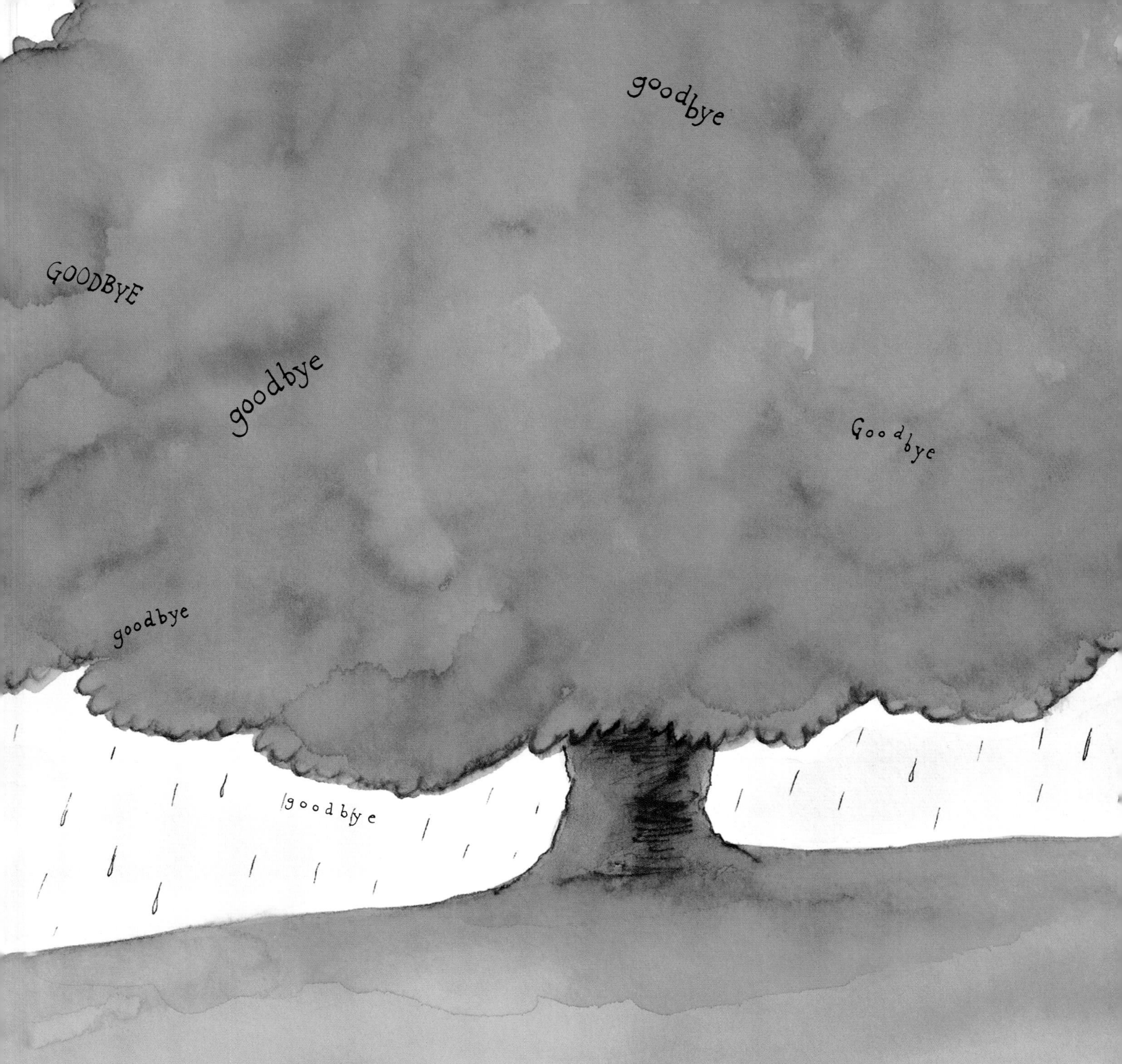

What did all the voices on the tree say?
What did the bear say, very loudly?
"Goodbye!"

Everyone had gone.
The tree stood quietly again.
"Hello, rain!" it said,
very, very quietly.